Dear Parents:

Congratulations! Your child is taking the first steps on an exciting journey. The destination? Independent reading!

STEP INTO READING® will help your child get there. The program offers five steps to reading success. Each step includes fun stories and colorful art or photographs. In addition to original fiction and books with favorite characters, there are Step into Reading Non-Fiction Readers, Phonics Readers and Boxed Sets, Sticker Readers, and Comic Readers—a complete literacy program with something to interest every child.

Learning to Read, Step by Step!

Ready to Read **Preschool–Kindergarten**
• big type and easy words • rhyme and rhythm • picture clues
For children who know the alphabet and are eager to begin reading.

Reading with Help **Preschool–Grade 1**
• basic vocabulary • short sentences • simple stories
For children who recognize familiar words and sound out new words with help.

Reading on Your Own **Grades 1–3**
• engaging characters • easy-to-follow plots • popular topics
For children who are ready to read on their own.

Reading Paragraphs **Grades 2–3**
• challenging vocabulary • short paragraphs • exciting stories
For newly independent readers who read simple sentences with confidence.

Ready for Chapters **Grades 2–4**
• chapters • longer paragraphs • full-color art
For children who want to take the plunge into chapter books but still like colorful pictures.

STEP INTO READING® is designed to give every child a successful reading experience. The grade levels are only guides; children will progress through the steps at their own speed, developing confidence in their reading.

Remember, a lifetime love of reading starts with a single step!

 Published in the United States by Random House Children's Books, a division of Penguin Random House LLC, 1745 Broadway, New York, NY 10019, and in Canada by Penguin Random House Canada Limited, Toronto, in conjunction with Disney Enterprises, Inc.

Step into Reading, Random House, and the Random House colophon are registered trademarks of Penguin Random House LLC.

Visit us on the Web!
StepIntoReading.com
rhcbooks.com

Educators and librarians, for a variety of teaching tools, visit us at RHTeachersLibrarians.com

ISBN 978-0-7364-3947-3 (trade) — ISBN 978-0-7364-8266-0 (lib. bdg.)
ISBN 978-0-7364-3948-0 (ebook)

Printed in the United States of America

10 9 8 7 6 5 4 3 2 1

Random House Children's Books supports the First Amendment and celebrates the right to read.

by Mary Tillworth

illustrated by the Disney Storybook Art Team

Random House New York

Aladdin is poor.
He steals bread to eat.
But he is also kind
and brave.

At night,
Aladdin looks at a palace.
He dreams of being rich.

One day, Aladdin
sees a young woman.
Her name is Jasmine.
She gives an apple
to a hungry child.

Jasmine cannot
pay for the apple.
The apple seller is angry!

Aladdin protects Jasmine.
Together, they run away.

Guards capture Aladdin!
They take him
to the dungeons.

Jasmine tries to stop them.

She is really a princess!

In the dungeon,
an old man frees Aladdin.

He asks Aladdin
to find a lamp.
Aladdin goes into a cave.
He gets the lamp.
He is trapped!

Aladdin

rubs the lamp.

A genie comes out!

The Genie can

grant three wishes.

Aladdin wishes

to be a prince!

Aladdin rides to the palace.
He finds Jasmine,
the Sultan, and
the evil Jafar.

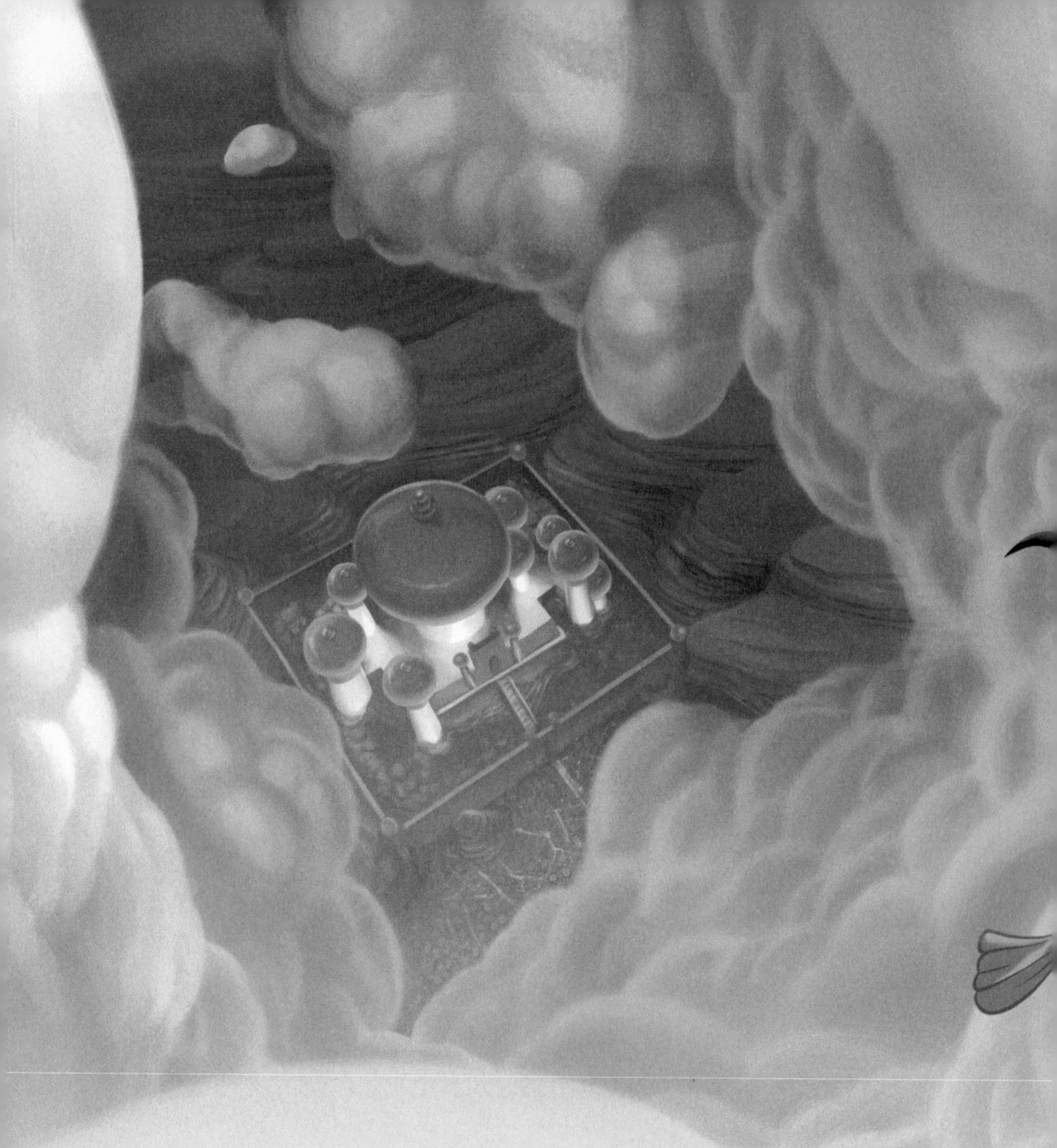

That night,
Aladdin takes Jasmine
on a magic carpet ride.

They have fun.

They fall in love!

They want to marry.

But Jafar wants
to marry Jasmine!
He throws Aladdin
into the sea.
Aladdin uses his
second wish.
The Genie saves him.

Jafar finds the magic lamp.

He wishes to be the sultan!

Jafar uses another wish.
He turns into a huge snake.
He squeezes Aladdin.

Aladdin tells Jafar
the Genie is more
powerful than he is.

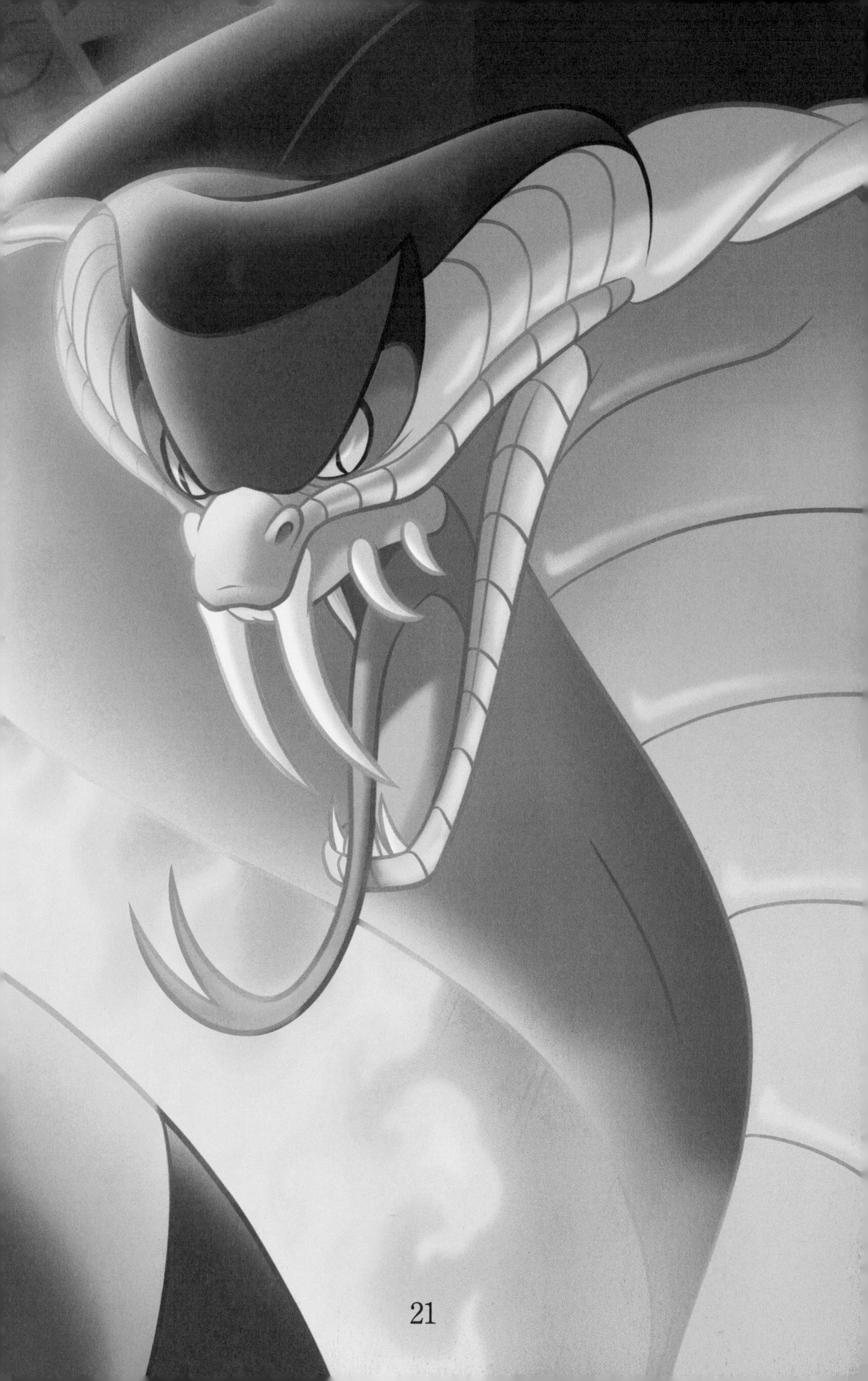

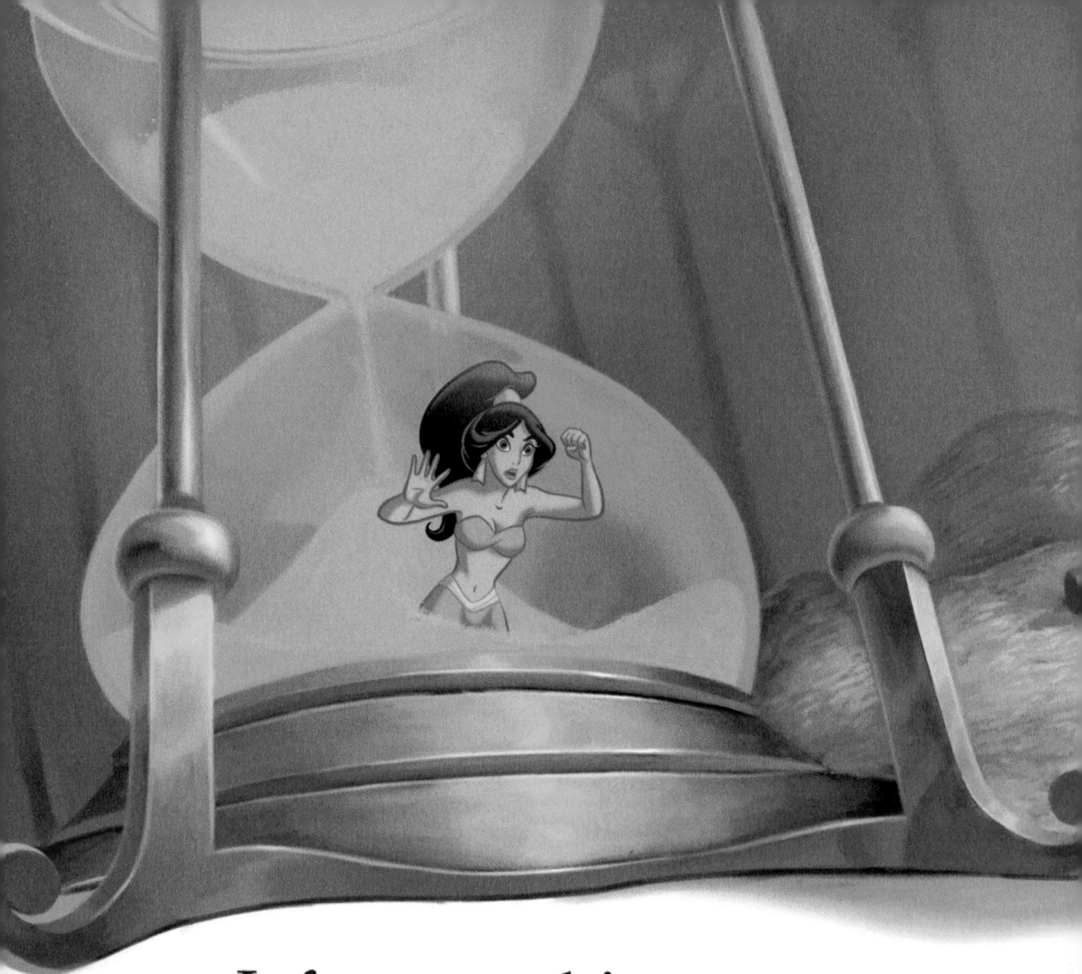

Jafar uses his
third wish.
He becomes a genie!
He traps Jasmine.
Aladdin saves her.

Jafar forgets
that every genie
lives in a lamp.
He is trapped
forever!

Aladdin uses his third wish.

He frees the Genie!

The Genie hugs everyone.

Kindness and bravery win!